For Thornton, my bug of Love
— L.M. (a.k.a. Puddin')

To Vincent
— C.G.

Text copyright © 2011 by Leslie Muir
Illustrations copyright © 2011 by Carrie Gifford

For information address Disney • Hyperion Books, 114 Fifth Avenue,

New York, New York 10011-5690.

First Edition

10 9 8 7 6 5 4 3 2 1

F850-6835-5-11015

Printed in Singapore

Reinforced binding

ISBN 978-1-4231-2756-7

Library of Congress Cataloging-in-Publication Data on file.

Visit www.disneyhyperionbooks.com

Barry B. Wary

by Leslie Muir

illustrated by Carrie Gifford

DISNEY·HYPERION BOOKS

NEW YORK

Barry B. Wary
loved to eat bugs—
with a succulent side dish
of sloshy–sweet slugs.
In a rose garden,
beneath a nut tree,
he sat crunching critters
much smaller than he.

Crispy click beetles! Mayflies in June!
A firefly soufflé by the light of the moon!

Hairy-kneed horseflies! A wee-teensy flea!
They all tasted scrumptious to young Barry B.

But eating alone
    just isn't much fun,
and Barry grew glum
    at his table for one.

He painted a sign—WANTED: A FRIEND

But friends won't come play when they think it's The End.

Then one sunny day,
    on pearl drops of dew,
a butterfly landed
    in Barry B.'s view.

Her flitter-by wings
   glowed glitter-sky blue.
Her curly antennae
   flopped cutely askew.

Barry was love struck.

He gazed from afar.

She'd captured his heart like a bug in a jar.

He loop-de-looped near and said with a gleam,
  "My dear, you look sweeter than cricket ice cream."

She let out an "Eeek!" and fluttered away

before he could give her a stinkbug bouquet.

He vowed and he pledged—
he'd prove his love true.

But how can you love
what you're dying to chew?

So Barry quit cold,
    stopped dining on bugs,
then sadly set free
    his delectable slugs.

He unplugged his zapper; but hardest to do—
he poured out his sauces for bug barbecue.

Barry B. Wary, bug-free as could be,
crunched upon rosebuds and sipped herbal tea.

He planted a present,
a nectar–sweet snack:
two butterfly bushes to
tempt his love back.

He listened for wing beats and searched the wide sky,
till night served up moon like a big glowworm pie.

Barry B. Wary lit candles galore,
set places for two,
and then worried some more.

His tummy did flip-flops, his fuzz lost its flair.
His night-vision goggles spied nothing but air.

Then Barry B. saw it!
The flash of a wing!
And out of the dark
came a flutter-fly thing.

Alas! His fair lady sailed into his sight,
did a spiraling nosedive right into his light.

Oh, no!

His poor sweetheart! A tear clogged his eye.
Was the love of his life now a blackened french fry?

But Barry B. smiled.
On closer inspection:

it was only a moth—
flame-grilled to perfection.

The End